READ SCI

Trucksgiving

TRUCKSGIVING

BY JON SCIESZKA

CHARACTERS AND ENVIRONMENTS DEVELOPED BY THE

DAVID SHANNON   **LOREN LONG**   **DAVID GORDON**

ILLUSTRATION CREW:

Executive Producer:

TOT
INDUSTRIES

Creative Supervisor: Nina Rappaport Brown ○ Drawings by: Dan Root ○ Color by: Antonio Reyna

Art Director: Karin Paprocki

READY-TO-ROLL

SIMON SPOTLIGHT

NEW YORK   LONDON   TORONTO   SYDNEY

SIMON SPOTLIGHT

An imprint of Simon & Schuster Children's Publishing Division
1230 Avenue of the Americas, New York, NY 10020

Copyright © 2010 by JRS Worldwide, LLC.

TRUCKTOWN AND JON SCIESZKA'S TRUCKTOWN and design are trademarks
of JRS Worldwide, LLC. All rights reserved, including the right of reproduction in
whole or in part in any form. SIMON SPOTLIGHT, READY-TO-READ, and colophon are
registered trademarks of Simon & Schuster, Inc. For information about special discounts for
bulk purchases, please contact Simon & Schuster Special Sales at 1-866-506-1949 or
business@simonandschuster.com. Manufactured in The United States of America 0810 LAK

First Edition 10 9 8 7 6 5 4 3 2 1

Library of Congress Cataloging-in-Publication Data

Scieszka, Jon.

Trucksgiving / by Jon Scieszka ; illustrated by the Design Garage
(David Shannon, Loren Long, David Gordon). — 1st ed.

p. cm. — (Ready-to-read) (Jon Scieszka's Trucktown)

Summary: The trucks of Trucktown create their own annual day of giving thanks.

1. Trucks—Fiction. 2. Thanksgiving Day—Fiction] I. Shannon, David, ill. II. Long, Loren, ill.
III. Gordon, David, 1965 Jan. 22- ill. IV. Design Garage. V. Title.

PZ7.S41267To 2010

[E]—dc22

2008030031

ISBN 978-1-4169-4146-0 (pbk)

ISBN 978-1-4169-4157-6 (hc)

Many years ago ...
the first trucks came
to Trucktown.

They dumped dirt.

They mixed cement.

They made roads.

They built Trucktown.

And they saw that
it was good.

They wanted a way to say thanks to every truck that helped.

They wanted a way to celebrate every year.

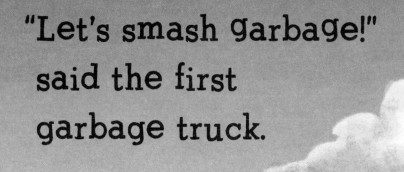

"Let's smash garbage!"
said the first
garbage truck.

"Ice cream? Ice cream? Ice cream?" said the first ice cream truck.

"I've got it," said the first Jack. "Every year we should have a ..."

And that is just what
the trucks do . . .